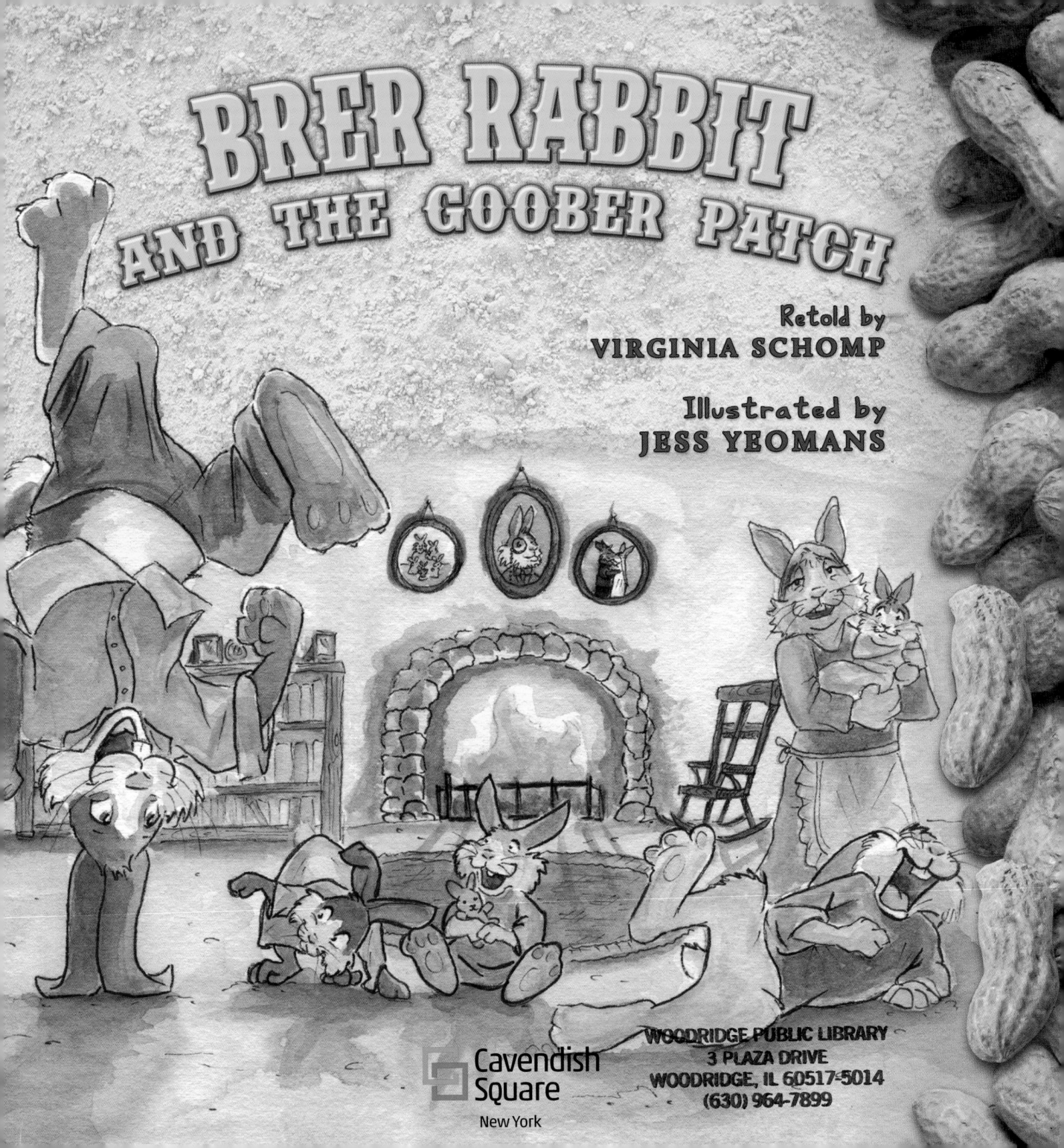

BRER RABBIT
AND THE GOOBER PATCH

Retold by
VIRGINIA SCHOMP

Illustrated by
JESS YEOMANS

Cavendish Square

New York

I N OLDEN TIMES, ANIMALS WERE A lot like people. They went to school. They went shopping. They had ball games and barbecues and birthday parties.

Like people, too, the animals didn't always get along. It seemed like somebody was always trying to trick somebody else. And who do you think was the tricksiest of all? Why, it was Brer Rabbit.

Now, Brer Rabbit wasn't bad. He was just full of mischief. He loved to play pranks on his friends, just for the fun of it. Like the time Brer Fox planted some goober peas. (That's another name for peanuts.) Brer Rabbit just *had* to have those goobers. And, of course, he'd need a trick or two to get himself out of trouble while he was nabbing them. . . .

3

One day, Brer Fox said to himself, "I believe I'll plant some goober peas!" And just like that, he set to work.

He cleared a patch of ground.
He hoed out the rows.
He planted the seeds.

Night after night, he toted those heavy buckets of water from the well.

4

It wasn't long before the leaves poked their heads out the ground just to see who was making all the racket.

Now, you might be wondering what Brer Rabbit was doing all this time. Truth is, that old rascal was just sitting and watching. He smiled when he saw Brer Fox sweating over the garden patch. He laughed when the peanuts began to ripen up. He winked his eye and sang a song to his little Rabbits.

Ti-yi! Tungalee!

I'll pick a pea, I'll eat a pea.

It grows in the ground, it grows so free.

Ti-yi! Those goober peas!

7

By and by, Brer Fox went to check on his garden. Great goodness! Somebody had been grabbling around among the vines! Somebody had been gobbling up the goobers!

Brer Fox was mighty mad. He had a pretty good idea who *somebody* was. But how could he catch that tricky old Rabbit?

He walked around the peanut patch. Looking. Looking. There it was—a hole in the fence! A hole just big enough for a smart-alecky Rabbit to wiggle through.

And right there, Brer Fox set his trap.

9

There was a young hickory tree growing next to the fence. Brer Fox bent it down and stuck the tip in the ground. He tied a rope in a loop and fixed it to the tree. He hung the loop in front of the fence, where it would catch someone slipping through the hole. Then he covered his trap with sticks and leaves to hide it.

"Ho-ho!" said Brer Fox. "Now we'll see who's been nabbing up my goobers!"

Early next morning, along came Brer Rabbit. He came skipping down the road, sassy as a jaybird. He stopped at the fence. He squeezed through the hole. His head passed through the loop, and his front legs followed. But not his belly. That was too fat. That was where the rope grabbed hold of him.

Brer Rabbit wriggled. He jiggled. He tried to pull himself free. All of a sudden—*boing!*—up flew the hickory tree. And there was Brer Rabbit, stuck between the heavens and the earth. There he hung, afraid he was going to fall—and even more afraid that he wasn't.

Well, sir, Brer Rabbit was in a fix, and he knew it. He worked his mind, trying to think up a likely tale to tell Brer Fox. Then—hang on! Who's that lumbering down the road? Why, it's his old friend Brer Bear!

Brer Rabbit hollered, "Howdy, Brer Bear!"

Brer Bear looked all around. He looked down. He looked up. He saw Brer Rabbit swinging in the breeze. "Heyo, Brer Rabbit. How are you this morning?"

Brer Rabbit grinned from ear to ear. "I'm fine *now*, thank you."

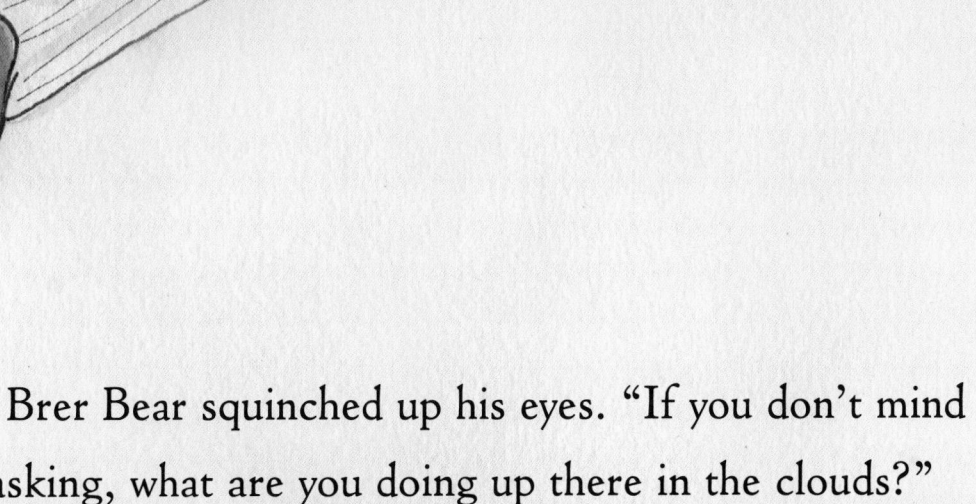

Brer Bear squinched up his eyes. "If you don't mind my asking, what are you doing up there in the clouds?"

"Oh, I'm earning myself a dollar a minute," Brer Rabbit said sort of careless like.

"A dollar a minute!"

"Yes, sir. Brer Fox is paying me to keep the crows out of his goober patch."

Now, Brer Bear had a big family, with lots of little cubs to feed. He sure could use some extra money. So he asked, "Do you think I could make a dollar a minute, too?"

Brer Rabbit thought it over. Then he answered most kindly. "Of course, friend. I think you'd make a fine scarecrow."

So Brer Rabbit showed Brer Bear how to bend down the tree. He loosened the rope and took it off his belly. It sure felt good to have his feet back on the ground! He pranced around, just as lively as a June cricket.

Then Brer Rabbit put the loop over Brer Bear's foot. They let go of the hickory tree. *Sproing!* Now Brer Bear was hanging up there in Rabbit's place.

"So long, friend. Watch out for those birds," said Brer Rabbit. "They can be tricky!" And he scampered off to Brer Fox's house.

"Brer Fox! Oh, Brer Fox!" he sang out. "Come on out here, Brer Fox, and I'll show you who's been stealing your goobers."

Brer Fox grabbed up his walking stick. He ran out of his house. He followed Brer Rabbit to the peanut patch. Sure enough, there was Brer Bear, caught in the trap. That old bear looked mighty peculiar swinging in the air, growling at crows!

"Howdy, Brer Fox," Brer Bear said. "How are you this fine— *Ouch! Ooooch!*"

"Oh yes! You are caught now, aren't you?" Brer Fox was hollering. "I'll show you what happens to goober-nabbers!" And he bopped Brer Bear over the head with his walking stick.

"But Brer Fox! I was just—"

Brer Rabbit jumped up and down. "Show him again, Brer Fox! Show him!" he shouted. And every time Brer Bear opened his mouth to explain, Brer Fox bopped him another one.

While all the bopping was going on, Brer Rabbit slipped away. He knew that Brer Bear would get loose soon enough. And when that old Bear was free, he just might go looking for the Rabbit that played such a slick trick on him.

Brer Rabbit scooted down the road. He came to a mud hole. He dove right in—*kerblunk!* Then he squatted down so only his eyeballs were sticking out.

25

It wasn't long before Brer Bear came
along. "Howdy, Brer Frog," he said. "Have
you seen Brer Rabbit?"

"He just went by," Brer Rabbit
said in a deep, froggy voice. "If
you hurry up, you'll catch him."

So Brer Bear galloped off down the road. Soon as he was out of sight, Brer Rabbit came out of the mud hole. He washed off in a puddle. He dried himself in the sun. Then he went skipping along home to his family. He told them the story of how he'd outfoxed Brer Fox and turned Brer Bear into a scarecrow. And all the little Rabbits laughed and laughed till they couldn't laugh anymore.

ABOUT BRER RABBIT

Brer Rabbit got his start in Africa. When Africans were taken to America as slaves, they brought their stories of the trickster-rabbit with them. These folktales were handed down over the years by slaves on southern plantations. The tales had a special meaning for the men, women, and children suffering under slavery. Brer Rabbit is small and weak, but he manages to outsmart many bigger, stronger animals. He reminds us that cleverness can win out over brute power.

Around 1880, a newspaperman named Joel Chandler Harris began to collect the Brer Rabbit stories. He wrote them down in a book called *Uncle Remus: His Songs and His Sayings*. The tales were so popular that Harris ended up publishing eight books, with more than 250 Brer Rabbit stories.

Our tale of Brer Rabbit is based on "Mr. Rabbit and Mr. Bear" and other stories in Uncle Remus: His Songs and His Sayings *by Joel Chandler Harris, first published in 1880.*

WORDS TO KNOW

brer A short way of saying "brother." The word comes from the southern United States, and it can be pronounced *brair* or *brur*.

folktales Traditional stories that have been handed down from earlier times. Folktales are made-up stories that happened "once upon a time."

goober peas A Southern nickname for peanuts.

grabbling Searching with the hands.

hickory tree A type of tall, straight tree that often has large, sweet-tasting nuts.

plantation A very large farm.

trickster A character who wins out through cleverness and trickery, instead of by fighting.

TO FIND OUT MORE

BOOKS

Amin, Karima. *The Adventures of Brer Rabbit and Friends: From Stories Collected by Joel Chandler Harris*. New York: DK Publishing, 2006.

Harris, Joel Chandler. *The Classic Tales of Brer Rabbit*. Retold by David Borgenicht. Philadelphia: Running Press Kids, 2008.

Websites

American Folklore: Brer Rabbit

http://americanfolklore.net/folklore/brer-rabbit/

Storyteller S. E. Schlosser retells funny stories about the adventures of Brer Rabbit.

BookHive: Zingertales

www.plcmc.org/bookhive/zingertales/default.asp?storyid=4

Storyteller Jackie Torrence shares a great retelling of the story "Brer Rabbit and the Well." You'll need the free RealPlayer plug-in to watch and listen.

The WHEEL Council: Storytellers

www.wheelcouncil.org/storytellers.html

The WHEEL Council offers tips on learning and telling stories. Click on "Brer Rabbit and the Mosquitos" to read about one of the many times the rascally rabbit outsmarted Brer Fox.

ABOUT THE AUTHOR

VIRGINIA SCHOMP has written more than seventy books for young readers on topics including dinosaurs, dolphins, American history, and ancient myths. She lives among the tall pines of New York's Catskill Mountain region. She enjoys hiking, gardening, watching old movies on TV and new anime online, and, of course, reading, reading, and reading.

ABOUT THE ILLUSTRATOR

JESS YEOMANS was born and raised on Long Island, New York, and grew up with a love of art and animals. She received her Illustration BFA at the Fashion Institute of Technology. She has been featured in many exhibits and has been awarded numerous awards and honors for her artwork.

Jess works as a freelance illustrator in Brooklyn. She enjoys drawing and painting, snowboarding, animals, cooking, and being outdoors. To see more of her work, visit www.jessyeomans.com.

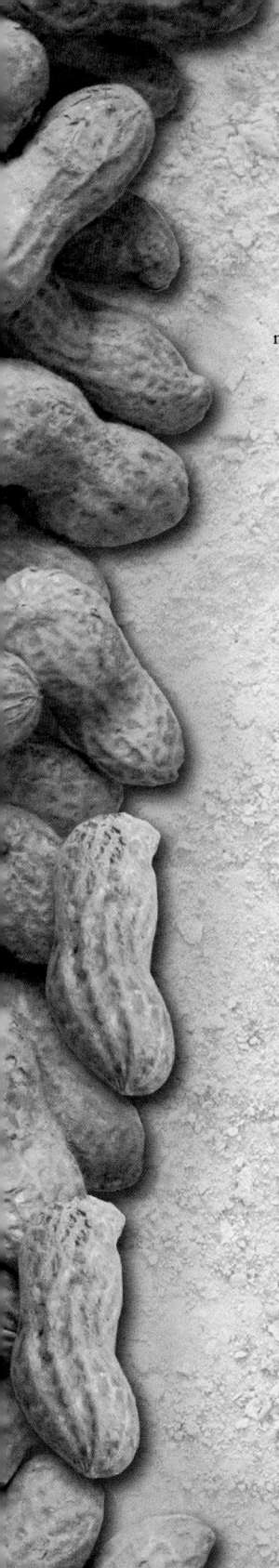

Published in 2014 by Cavendish Square Publishing, LLC
303 Park Avenue South, Suite 1247, New York, NY 10010

Copyright © 2014 by Cavendish Square Publishing, LLC

First Edition

Website: cavendishsq.com

This publication represents the opinions and views of the author based on his or her personal experience, knowledge, and research. The information in this book serves as a general guide only. The author and publisher have used their best efforts in preparing this book and disclaim liability rising directly or indirectly from the use and application of this book.

CPSIA Compliance Information: Batch #WS13CSQ

All websites were available and accurate when this book was sent to press.

LIBRARY OF CONGRESS CATALOGING-IN-PUBLICATION DATA
Schomp, Virginia.
Brer Rabbit and the goober patch / Virginia Schomp.
p. cm. — (American legends and folktales)
Summary: Brer Rabbit steals peanuts, or goobers, from the garden patch Brer Fox has sweated over then tricks Brer Bear into taking the blame.
Includes bibliographical references and index.
ISBN 978-1-60870-439-2 (hardcover) ISBN 978-1-62712-014-2 (paperback) ISBN 978-1-60870-605-1 (ebook)
[1. African Americans—Folklore. 2. Animals—Folklore. 3. Folklore—United States.] I. Harris, Joel Chandler, 1848-1908. Brer Rabbit and the goober patch. II. Title.
PZ8.1.S3535Bre 2014
398.2—dc23
[E]
2012010545

Printed in the United States of America

EDITOR: Deborah Grahame-Smith
ART DIRECTOR: Anahid Hamparian   SERIES DESIGNER: Kristen Branch